LOOKING FOR ME

Betsy R. Rosenthal

* * * *

Houghton Mifflin

Houghton Mifflin Harcourt

Boston   New York   2012

Houghton Mifflin is an imprint of Houghton Mifflin Harcourt
Publishing Company.

www.hmhbooks.com

The text of this book is set in Centaur MT.
The photographs are courtesy of the Paul family.
Glossary on pages 164–165.

Library of Congress Cataloging-in-Publication Control Number 2011017124

ISBN 978-0-547-61084-9

Manufactured in TK
TK 10 9 8 7 6 5 4 3 2 1
45XXXXXXXXXX

* * * *

To my wonderfully loving and selfless mom,
for sharing a lifetime of stories with me

Edith of No Special Place

I'm just plain Edith.
I'm number four,
and should anyone care,
I'm eleven years old,
with curly black hair.

Squeezed / between / two / brothers,
Daniel and Ray,
lost in a crowd,
will I ever be more
than just plain Edith,
who's number four?

In my overcrowded family
I'm just another face.
I'm just plain Edith
of no special place.

Always One More

I saw these wooden nesting dolls in a store,

the kind where you don't know how many dolls

there are altogether until you start

opening them up,

and there's always

one more inside,

sort of like

my family.

Family Portrait, Baltimore, 1936

We're lined up:
girl boy, girl boy, girl boy, girl boy, girl boy,

and in the middle of us all, Dad,
who ordered us to smile
right before the Brownie clicked,
standing stiff as a soldier,
no smile on *his* face,

and Mom's beside him,
a baby in her arms
and in her rounded belly
another one,

just a trace.

Inspector Bubby

When Mom goes to the hospital
to have this new baby,
us older kids
watch the younger ones
and keep the house clean.

We think we're doing okay
until Dad's mother, Bubby Anne,
comes over
and runs her finger across the top
of the china cabinet
that we couldn't even reach,

just to show us the dust
we've left behind.

There Goes That Theory

Nobody asked *my* opinion
about having another sister or brother.
But if someone had,

I would have asked
for another little sister,
even though I was sure

this new baby
in Mom's belly
had to be a boy.

How could I be so sure?
Because the last girl she had
was my sister Annette.

Sometime after Annette came along,
Mom collapsed
and Dad rushed her to the hospital,

where they took out one of her ovaries
(part of her baby-making equipment,
Bubby Anne told us).

So my sisters and I thought
it must have been
the girl-making one

because since the surgery
Mom has had nothing but boys —
my brothers Lenny, Melvin, Sol, and Jack.

But now this baby in Mom's belly
turned out to be Sherry.
And that's the end

of our ovary theory.

Now We're Even

Maybe Mom and Dad
wanted one last one
to even things up.
With six boys
and now six girls,
maybe they're done.

I guess there's really
no way of knowing,
but I sure hope
our family's
all done growing.

Some People Don't Understand About a Big Family

My friends Connie and Eunice
love coming to my house.
To them it seems like
we're always having a party.

But I'd rather go to their houses,
where there's room to move around
without bumping into anybody

and you *never*
have to stand in line
to use the bathroom.

I Wonder What It Would Be Like

To sleep by myself
in this bed
that holds three
with all of the covers
to cover
just me.

To spread my arms wide
and lie
at a slant
with no other bodies
to say
that I can't.

To lie
on a pillow,
no feet in my face;
I'd lie awake nights
just feeling the space.

Keeping the Days Straight

Since it's summertime
and we aren't back in school yet,
I keep forgetting what day it is.

So my brother Raymond
teaches me the trick
of checking what Mom's making for dinner.

Mondays are *milkhik*,
Tuesdays, liver;
Wednesdays are macaroni casserole days,
Thursdays are meat,
and Fridays we eat a Shabbos feast
of chicken, chopped liver, and soup.
Saturdays we have what's left,
and Sundays Dad brings home deli.

So the day of the week
all depends
on what's inside my belly.

Why Can't Summer Last Forever?

Summer means
we're outside,
trying to cool off.
So my little brother Melvin
grabs my hand
and we run by the garden hose
that Mom's waving around.
We scream with glee
as she hoots and sprays us
with its misty breath.

Summer means
trips to the shore with Dad,
where we all play tag
with the waves
and build castles in the sand
and then, on the way home,
stop for kosher dogs,
lathered with mustard,
like shaving cream on a man's face.

Summer means
matinees at the Roxy Theatre
on weekdays,
not just weekends,
and taking my brothers and sisters
to the park
to play dodge ball
and horseshoes
and hum in the kazoo band.

Why can't summer last forever?

Lucky Lenny

Last Sunday
when Dad took us to swim in the bay
at Workmen's Circle Lodge,
my little brother Lenny slipped
on a plum pit in the pavilion
and broke both his legs.

He's in the hospital now,
getting loads of comic books,
marbles, and card games
and more candy buttons and chocolate licorice
than he could ever eat,
and the nurses are fluffing up his pillows
and bringing him grape soda all the time.
He's even making new friends,
playing war and go fish
with the man in the next bed.

Today when we went to swim,
I looked as hard as I could
for my own
plum pit.

One Summer Night

My little sister Marian is missing again,
so Dad packs some of us into his Hudson
(we can't all fit)
and we drive around until we finally find Marian
in the park,
bouncing her little paddle board and ball,
not even noticing the dark
at all.

When we get home,
Dad uses Marian's paddle,
but not on the ball,
and she doesn't act like she's sorry
at all.

Goodbye to Summer

When Dad's mother, Bubby Anne,
gives us all pairs of new socks
to wear to school,
it's time to say goodbye to summer.

When Mom's mom, Bubby Etta,
reaches into her shopping bag
full of crayons, jacks, and candy
and hands each of us
"a little something special
to start off the new school year,"
it's time to say goodbye to summer.

But I wish it wasn't.
Now I'll have to go to school all day
instead of swimming
at the Patterson Park pool
and playing stickball
with Daniel and his friends
and taking Melvin to the Roxy
to see the Popeye cartoons.

I'll have to get up early,
even before the sun rubs the sleep
out of its eyes.
I'll have to face math tests
and spelling bees and homework,
and the weather will turn dreary and stormy
like in a scary movie.

I know it's time to say goodbye to summer,
but I'd much rather be saying hello.

I Wish I Had New
Back-to-School Clothes

But in my family
we wear
hand-me-down
down
down
down
downs.

The First Day of Sixth Grade

My new teacher, Miss Connelly,
is making us write a poem
about our family.
It's not exactly fair
because mine will have to be really, really long.

I'll start with Dad,
who only wanted lots of kids
so he could put us all to work
at his diner when we're old enough.

Then Mom,
who works hard all day at the diner
and all night at home,
but still finds time to dance with us
and make us caramel apples on a stick,
no matter how tired she is.

Then there's Sylvia, my oldest sister,
who never tells on me
if I sneak a slice of pie at the diner
when Dad's not there,

and Mildred, the queen of us all,
who likes to wave the candy and flowers
in our faces
that she gets from her dozens
of boyfriends,

and Daniel, the favorite son,
who would walk the plank for Mom
if she asked him to,
and whenever he earns a little money,
he buys something special just for her.

Then there's Raymond, who I help
with schoolwork,
although he sometimes skips school
and always seems to get spanked
more than the rest of us,

and Marian, who is never done playing,
so I have to drag her home for dinner
while she screams so loud the neighbors
think I'm murdering her,

and Annette, who follows me around
all the time
and cries waterfall tears
when I try to lose her,

and Lenny, Sol, and Jack,
the three musketeers,
who are always looking for adventure,
always finding trouble,

and Melvin, my very favorite,
who walks to the bakery with me
to get the Sabbath challah,
holding on to my pinkie finger
with his little hand,
his brown ringlets bouncing
from side to side.

And finally, there's Sherry,
who's just a baby in a carriage
and the last child
(I hope!)
of my way-too-big family.

Poem Correction

"You left someone important
out of this poem, Edith,"
Miss Connelly tells me after class.

"Who?" I ask,
keeping my eyes glued to my shoes.

"You," she says.
"Where are *you* in this family?"

"Number four," I say,
"in between Daniel and Ray."

"Nothing more?" she asks.
"I didn't want to write about me," I say.

"Why not?" she asks.
"Because," I blurt out, "I don't know
who I am in my big family."

"Maybe you can go home and think about
who you are," she says.

So I walk out the door,
wondering who I am
besides number four.

Still Searching

After school
Mom's looking right at me,
fumbling for my name,
"Marian, Sylvia, Mildred, Annette . . .
I mean Edith,
can you empty the ice pan?"

If my mother
doesn't even know who I am,
how am I supposed to?

Who I Am

While I'm changing Sherry's diaper,
Miss Connelly's question
is rolling around in my head like a marble,
and I start to get an idea
about who I am in this family.

It has to do with the nickname
everyone in the neighborhood
calls me —
"the good little mother"—

because while Mom's at work,
I'm always pushing a carriage
or changing
or playing with
or feeding
one
or two
or three
of my little sisters and brothers.

When I take them to Patterson Park,
I like to pretend they're my own children,
holding them when they cry,
patting their backs,
and saying, "My baby, my baby . . ."

I guess sometimes I'd rather
be jumping double dutch
or playing stickball with my friends,
but except for the stinky diapers,
I sure do like being
"the good little mother."

An Undeserved Nickname

Mom's not home yet from Dad's diner,
and here I am,
right in the middle
of changing Sherry's diaper,
trying not to prick myself
with the safety pin,
when Jack starts whimpering
because he wet his pants.

Then Sherry starts crying
and Jack's blubbering
and tugging on my shirt.

I need some clean pants quick,
so I send Annette to bring me a pair
from the cellar,
where I hung them on the line
this morning.

"What's taking so long?
Just bring the pants already!"
I yell to Annette.
Jack and Sherry are both wailing
so loud it sounds like an ambulance siren.

When Annette finally comes back,
she tells me there aren't any pants
down there.
I slap her face so hard
my hand leaves a print
on her cheek.

She bursts into tears.
"But, Edie, I couldn't go down to the cellar.
It was pitch black
and I heard scary noises
coming from there."

I see the tears dripping down her face,
and suddenly I don't feel very much
like a good little mother
anymore.

If Only . . .

I were an only child
like my cousin Sonny,
I'd have the bathtub all to myself,
dipping my toes into water
as piping hot as a cup of tea
and so clean and clear you could drink it.

But instead, I get in line
to climb into the tub
after Mildred, Daniel,
Marian, Ray, and sometimes Annette
have all taken their turns.

And by then
the water's as murky brown
as a mud puddle
and not
even one bit
still hot.

Even *I* Get in Trouble Sometimes

My brothers and sisters think
that I'm a goody two-shoes,
and most of the time
they're right.

But sometimes
I'm not a goody anything.
I mean I don't disappear like Marian,
don't skip school like Raymond;
I'm not out looking for trouble
like Lenny, Sol, and Jack.

But sometimes
trouble finds *me*.

Like today,
when the iceman came in the morning
and shoved the frozen block
into our icebox
with tongs that look like tigers' teeth.

By afternoon, when it was hotter
than blazes,
I went into the kitchen
to make myself a lettuce and tomato sandwich
and found a puddle on the floor.

Mom got back from the diner,
and as soon as she came into the kitchen,
she yelled,
"Whose turn was it to empty the ice pan?"
and because
it wasn't a wait-till-your-*father*-gets-home yell,
and because Mom would never hit me,
I confessed to the crime.

A Wait-Till-Your-*Father*-Gets-Home! Yell

We're in the girls' bedroom,
scooping out globs of oily peanut butter
straight from the jar,
rolling it between our palms
into smooth balls,

aiming at our targets
across the room,
girls against boys.
But somebody ducks —
a ball splats against the wallpaper.

Now the battle's in full swing —
brown bullets flying
across the room,
our brand-new wallpaper
looking more and more
like a leopard spotted with grease marks.

We're laughing so hard
that our bellies are aching
and so loud
that nobody even hears
the footsteps.

"Wait till your father gets home!"
Mom screams,
and we all know
that at the very least,
it's the last time
there'll ever be peanut butter
in *our* house.

It Could Be Worse

I wonder if our peanut butter battle
will bring
the sting of the belt today.

Dad uses his belt
for more than just holding up
his pants.

Dad uses his belt
when he's so bursting with anger
that shouting isn't enough.

Dad uses his belt
most often
on Ray.

Dad's never used his belt
on me.

And I
want to keep it that way.

When He Comes Home

Even though Mom's face is angry red
and the brand-new wallpaper
is covered with oily battle scars,
Dad keeps his belt
right where it belongs —
in the loops of his pants.

Maybe his hand would get too tired
whipping so many bottoms.
Maybe there are just too many of us
to hit.
Maybe this is what
safety in numbers
really means.

I Know Who I'm Not

Mildred and I
are taking toe-dancing lessons
on Saturdays.
Last week the teacher told Mom
that Mildred
was the dancer in the family.
So Mom bought ballet slippers
for her,
but I still have to stand
on my toes
in saddle oxfords.

I don't complain one bit,
but when I see Mildred
pirouetting around the parlor,
I feel like doing something
Marian would do —
like stomping my saddle oxfords
right on Mildred's dainty ballerina toes.

A Bad Fairy Tale

It's housecleaning day,
and Mildred's making me
do all her chores.
Again.

I'm sweeping the steps
and wiping the windows for her.
Again.

And I'm taking care of baby Sherry
while she's busy painting her toenails.
Again.

Mom and Dad say
I always have to do
what my older sisters and brother
tell me to,
but I'm sick of Mildred
making me do all her chores.

And if I don't,
she'll tell on me.
I ought to tell on *her*.

But Mom has enough to worry about
and Dad wouldn't care.
I'd get in trouble
for bothering him.

There's no one to tell,
so I escape
and run next door
to Connie's house.

When Mildred starts screeching, "Edie!
Come change Sherry's diaper!"
Connie stuffs me into a giant storage trunk,
where I've hidden before.
I'm meat stuffed into cabbage.
"She'll never find you in here,"
Connie says.

A second later
I hear Mildred stomp in,
demanding to know where I am.
"I haven't seen her," Connie's mom says,
"but you're welcome to look around."

I get comfortable,
take my shoes off in the trunk,
and keep still,
trying hard not to giggle
until Mildred finally leaves.

When the coast is clear,
I sneak back over to our house,
but my cold feet remind me
that I left my shoes at Connie's.

Before I can even go back to get them,
Mildred spies me
and hands me the crying baby
with her stinky diaper still on,
like she's some kind of present.

And I feel like Cinderella
before she ever met
her fairy godmother.

Mom's Birthday Surprise

I've been saving the money
I've earned from odd jobs,
like polishing the neighbors' steps,
so I could buy Mom
a birthday present —
a potted geranium,
her favorite flower.

I hide the plant
behind my back
and find Mom
in the kitchen.
Sylvia's there, too,
and so are Mildred and Marian.

"Happy birthday!" I cry,
and hand her the geranium.
Then she cups my cheek lightly
with her hand,
kisses my forehead,
and thanks me
as she puts the plant
on the long kitchen table

next to the three others
just like it.

A September Swim with My Favorite Little Brother

I'm sitting in class,
dripping from this Indian summer heat,
trying hard to pay attention
to Miss Connelly's lesson,
when all of a sudden
a waterfall of rain gushes down outside.

As soon as the afternoon bell rings,
I dash home,
the rain matting down my black curls,
and when I open the door,
Melvin yells, "Eeediff . . . !"
and wraps his arms around my legs.

I run upstairs to peel off my wet clothes
and put on my bathing suit.
Then I pull Melvin's swimming trunks on him
and grab his hand.

We race to the end of the street,
where the rainwater doesn't drain
and it's three feet deep,
and we jump in together,
still holding hands.

Melvin starts flapping his arms
in the water like a bird
and laughs while he sprays me
with his wings,
and I hold both his hands
and swish him around me
like a motorboat
going faster and faster and faster.

I wish I could keep holding
Melvin's hands,
swishing him around
in our own private street pool
forever.

Open Wide

Maybe the swim
was a dumb thing to do,
because I'm home with a cold
and Melvin's sick, too.

We can stand the sneezing
and noses that don't stop dripping
and even the tea with lemon and whiskey
Mom makes us keep sipping.

But when Mom gets the castor oil
and says, "Open wide,"
Melvin and I
try to run off and hide.

It's too late for that.
Here comes the spoon.
"Drink it down," Mom says.
"You'll feel better soon."

It tastes so awful,
Melvin starts to cry.
"It's not that bad," I tell him,
even though it's a lie.

Maybe the swim
was a dumb thing to do,
because now we're both sick
from castor oil, too.

Bubby Anne's Store

When Melvin and I are over our colds,
I take him and Sol
to visit Bubby Anne.
She lives above her dry goods store,
and when she hears
the bell tinkling over the opened door,
she comes down
to help the customers.

To spare her legs
the walk downstairs
when we stop by,
as soon as we open the tinkling door,
we yell upstairs
to the second floor,
"It's nobody!"

How We Got Our Name

Bubby Anne's last name is Polansky.
I would've been Edith Polansky except
that Dad, who was a Polansky
for most of his life,
followed Uncle Jake
who says he changed his name
for business' sake
from Polansky
to Paul.

I'm glad we changed our name
to Paul.
It's easier to say
and to spell,
and it rhymes with lots of words
like wall
and hall
and fall
and call
and even
with my little brother Sol.

I'm glad
we changed our name
to Paul,
because nothing
rhymes with Polansky.

At Lunchtime Every Tuesday

When Dad goes to see his mother,
my Bubby Anne,
she serves him gefilte fish
with the bones still in it,
but he says it doesn't matter,
because she's a good businesswoman.

She's too busy at her dry goods store
to come to our house much,
so she sends Dad home
with her bony gefilte fish.

But we don't mind
because when we visit her,
she gives us nickels
and new socks.

Bubby Anne always says she'll never live
with any of her children.
"It's not good for two women
to be in one kitchen," she says.

But if only she would invite
my other *bubby*—
Mom's mother—into her kitchen,
maybe she could learn a thing or two
about cooking!

Keeping Kosher, Maryland-Style

Most of the kids are Catholic
who live on our street,
so they don't worry much
about what they eat.

But we aren't allowed
to mix milk with our meat,
or eat bacon, shrimp, crab,
or pickled pigs' feet.

And we use separate dishes
for milk foods and meat
and paper plates for crab cakes
('cause sometimes we cheat).

Trying to Be Polite at Eunice's House

Eunice and I mostly go
to *my* house after school
because she thinks it's more fun
than a circus.
But today we go to Eunice's
for a change
(which I like because it's nice and quiet).

She asks if I'm hungry,
and of course, I say yes
because I love to eat
(maybe too much).

She offers me kielbasa,
a Polish treat,
and I say, "No thanks,"
even though my stomach
is growling for it.

"How about a ham and cheese?" she says,
lifting her eyebrows.
"No, thank you," I say,
and worry she'll think
I'm the pickiest eater
in all of Baltimore.

"Don't like ham and cheese either?"
she asks,
with her hands planted on her hips.
"Nope," I say,
willing my stomach to hush up.

"What *do* you like?" she asks.
"Everything else," I say,
and I don't try to explain
why I can't eat pig,
because I came over to Eunice's house
to play.
I don't want my Jewish eating rules
to get in the way.

My Dumb Neighbor

Peggy Schmidt,
this new girl in the neighborhood,
is coming over to play
for the very first time.
I open the front door
and find her staring up
at our doorjamb.
"What's that thing?" she points.
"It's a mezuzah —
a Jewish thing," I tell her.

Then we go down to the cellar
to cut out paper doll clothes
and she's looking at me
with eyes wider than bicycle tires.
She comes right up to me
and starts poking her fingers
through the black curls
on the top of my head.
"What are you doing?" I ask.
"I'm looking for your horns," she says.

I'm not usually a shouter,
but I'm sure you could hear my voice
in the next county
yelling, "WHAT?"

Mom told me
that there are dumb people who think
that Jews have horns.
Only I never thought
I'd meet one

in my own house.

After School

Jimmy Lenchowski chases me
like an angry storm
and calls me "Jew bagel"
and screams at me
about how I killed Jesus Christ.

When he comes after me,
my stomach starts jumping rope
and I run like a rabbit
to escape his attack,

run all the way home
and never look back.

Maybe I Should Be More Like Marian

Say what I feel,
do what I want,
act on a dare.

Maybe I should be more like Marian.

Go where I want,
Make myself heard,
never be scared.

The Memory Dance

Bubby Etta comes to visit
and I ask her to tell us a
how-it-was-in-the-old-country story.

First she closes her eyes,
to see the past better, I guess.
Then her body starts to sway
like she's doing a memory dance
and the words,
in her old-country accent,

                             come

                                    tumbling

                                            out.

"In Russia I was a midwife.
One night a man knocked on my door.
'The baby's coming; the baby's coming!' he yelled.

"I rushed to his house with him.
It vas outside of our village,
where no Jews were allowed.

"I brought out the baby from the mother
and then I brought another baby from the mother
and then I brought the third baby from the mother.

"The man was so shocked
he fainted.

"I brought thousands of babies into this world
and never lost even one.

"They trusted me
with their babies,
but they called my people
zhyd.

"They trusted me
with their babies,
but they wouldn't let the Jews
study at university
or vote
or learn Russian in school
or live where we wanted.

"They took us from our homes
in the middle of the night
and marched us through the streets,
and sometimes they beat us . . .

"but they trusted me
with their babies."

Bubby stops swaying,
opens her eyes,
wipes the wetness from her cheeks,
and says,

*"Here in America, I can bring babies into this world
and I can live where I want
and I am not afraid
to be who I am."*

Even in America

Today after school,
when Jimmy Lenchowski
starts yelling
about how I killed Jesus Christ,
I think about the story
Bubby told me yesterday
and how in America
she doesn't have to be afraid
to be who she is.

Well, neither do I.
So for the first time
I yell right back at Jimmy,
"I couldn't have killed Jesus,
because I wasn't even born then,
but my brothers are going to kill you
if you don't leave me alone!
And believe me,
I have a lot of them."

Jimmy's eyebrows shoot up
and he stands there
looking like he just got punched.
Then he turns and runs
as if my brothers are at his heels.

And after that,
I'm not one bit scared
of Jimmy Lenchowski
anymore.

Maybe I'm Not Cut Out to Be the Good Little Mother

There's always someone in this family
who needs something from me,
always someone pestering me.

I'm just trying to do my homework
at the kitchen table
when Annette asks me to cut a kaiser roll
for her.

Eager to get back to my homework,
I snatch the knife
and slice more than the kaiser roll.

Suddenly blood's gushing out
of my finger
and a piece of it's dangling
like a yo-yo on a string.

Annette's pointing at it,
screaming, "Blood!"
like my head's been chopped off.
Then she runs for Raymond,
who rushes me to the corner druggist.

The druggist wraps my finger
tightly in cotton
and holds it
till the blood stops spurting.

I think I'll stay
far away from kaiser rolls
for a while
(and maybe little sisters
who need me to do things for them, too),
at least until my finger
stops hurting.

Raymond Gets into Trouble

A postcard comes home
from Hebrew school.
"Raymond Paul absent for a week," it says.
"Where were you?" Dad asks him.
Raymond tells him the truth.
"I was watching the serials
at the Roxy Theatre."

"I'll fix you, Raymond," Dad says.
Then he tells me to go upstairs
and get my brightest dress.
I come down with the rainbow one.

Dad makes him put it on
and go outside
when it's time for his buddies to gather
in the back alley.

That fixes Raymond, all right.
He decides he looks much better
in Hebrew school
than in my rainbow dress.

Not Everything Can Be Mended

I'm squished in bed
between Marian and Annette,
thinking about Ray
and how his friends were all snickering
when they saw him
and how I wouldn't want to be Ray.
And even though it's really late,
I just can't sleep,
so I go downstairs.

Mom's sitting in the overstuffed armchair,
staring right through the picture
on the wall
of her father in Russia.
She has a threaded needle in one hand,
a button in the other,
and a crumpled shirt on her lap.
A pile of clothes lies next to her,
waiting to be mended.

And I don't know why,
but she starts telling me
this story that I never heard before
about Bubby Etta,
about how she divorced Mom's father
and married Jacob,
about how she put Mom in a baby basket
and left her on Mom's father's doorstep
in Russia,
while Bubby Etta sailed for America
with her new husband, Jacob,

and promised to send for Mom
as soon as she had the money for a ticket,
but it took thirteen years
before Bubby sent the ticket.

That's when I make up my mind
to stop talking to Bubby Etta
for *at least*
thirteen years.

Staying Mad

After school the next day
I'm on my way past
Bubby Etta's house
on Baltimore Street.

I think I smell her chicken schmaltz soup
with pieces of challah floating in it
that she makes special for me
when I stop by,

or maybe she's baking her pirogen
with raisins and nuts,
soaked in so much honey
that when I take a bite,
it drizzles down my chin.

She's probably wearing her housedress
that looks like a flower garden,
and if I went inside,
I bet she'd wrap me in her hugging arms
the minute she saw me.

I'd stay in those arms
for a while,
since it's hard to get hugs in my house.

Then she'd want to know all about
what I've been doing,
and she'd listen hard,
like I was the only grandchild she had.

I'd talk for a while
because good listeners
are hard to find in my house.

But I won't stop in
on Baltimore Street
today.

No.
Today
I'll walk right by.

A Bad Sign

When I finally get home,
my head still filled with thoughts
of all I'm missing at Bubby's,
I see a sign posted in front
of our row house —
AUCTION.

I go inside to ask Mom what it means,
and she tells me
that our house will be sold
because Dad loaned some money
to Bubby Etta's husband, Jacob,
and he couldn't pay Dad back.

"How can we lose our house
just because Zayde Jacob
couldn't pay Dad back?"
I ask.

Now I'm even madder
at Bubby Etta.
First she leaves Mom in Russia
and now her husband
leaves *us* without a house.

My insides feel like I swallowed
a whole bucketful of needles,
and I try not to cry.
"Where will we live?" I ask Mom.
But I don't get any answers.

That Night

Dad writes a letter
to President Roosevelt,
asking for his help.

And I start picturing all of us kids
being sent to an orphanage
or sleeping in the diner.

So I go inside and start praying
as hard as I can
that we'll get to keep our house.

I never prayed for anything before,
but this sure is worth praying
my heart out for.

Somebody Listened

It's only been ten days
since Dad sent the letter
and I prayed my heart out,
so I don't know
who answered our prayers first,
God or the president,
but when I get home from school today,
the auction sign is gone
and the house I've lived in
my whole entire life
is still ours.
I feel tons lighter
and want to hug and kiss somebody,
maybe even President Roosevelt,
who has become my family's
hero.

An Explanation, Sort Of

When Mom gets home from work,
before she starts cooking dinner,
she takes me aside.

"Bubby Etta tells me
you haven't stopped by
to see her lately," she says.
"I don't want to see her," I say.
"She left you in Russia,
and Zayde Jacob almost
left *us* without a house."

"Edith, you must stop
being mad at Bubby Etta," she says.
"But how could she leave you behind?"
I ask,
getting mad all over again.

"I was a baby, too little to travel.
Many making that journey
died on the way," she says.
"Bubby did the best
that she could."

"Would you ever leave me behind?"
I ask Mom.
"I would never
leave any of my children
behind," she says.

And I believe her.

Disappearing Act

Today I take the long way home
so I won't have to pass
by Bubby Etta's house
since I'm still not
ready to forgive her.

When I get home,
Melvin runs to greet me,
his eyes as wide as potato latkes.
He grabs my arm with his sticky hands.

"Come 'ere!" he yells
as he pulls me toward the parlor.
"What is it, Melvin?" I ask.

Then I hear a tiny voice cry out,
"We're here inside!"
"Where?" I call back.

"In dere," Melvin says,
pointing to the folded-up bed,
and all I see sticking out . . .
is Jackie's puny head.

They're Lucky I Found Them

Lenny, Sol, and Jack
said Mom left them sleeping
on the sofa bed,
or so she thought,
and ran to the store.

But after she left,
they started to bounce
and bounce
and bounce some more.

Then the bed closed up
and they were stuck
until I came home
and changed their luck.

I Wonder

If a sofa bed swallowed *me* up
like a hungry tiger,
would anyone care?

With twelve kids to look after,
would Mom and Dad notice?

Would *anyone* notice
if I wasn't there?

It's Hard to Stay Mad at Bubby Etta

Since it's so cold outside,
I don't want to take the long way home,
so I stop by today
to warm up a little,
but really to ask Bubby Etta how
she could have left Mom in Russia
for so many years.

She tells me that she tried
to bring her over sooner
and that it hurt bad in her *kishkes*
to be so far away from her.

She says she saved the money
people gave her
for bringing their babies
into the world
so she could bring her baby
to America.

"My husband,
he used that money to bet on horses,"
she says,
"but he always lost,
and that's why it took so long
to buy your mother's ticket."

So
it was really
my step-*zayde* Jacob's fault!
I never liked him
anyway.

It's Our New Year

Mom says Rosh Hashanah
is the gift of a new start for each one of us
and that we need to think hard
about the bad things we've done all year.

I bet every year Bubby Etta thinks about
what she did a long time ago —
leaving Mom in Russia.
And I hope Zayde Jacob thinks about
how it was his fault
Mom couldn't come here sooner.

But I have to think about what I've done.
So for starters,
I think about how
I let the ice pan overflow
so many times
and threw those greasy peanut butter balls
against the new wallpaper
and especially
how I slapped Annette so hard
it left a mark.

Mom says we need to
tell the people we've hurt
that we're sorry
and promise to do better
in the new year.

She says that on Rosh Hashanah
God hears our apologies
and decides what will happen to each of us
in the coming year.

So I'd better hurry up and get started
saying I'm sorry.
I don't want God
to get the wrong idea about me.

Like We Do Every Year
on Rosh Hashanah

With our new clothes
from Bubby Anne's store
(hats and white gloves for the girls,
suits and ties for the boys)
and our new starts,

we walk to Bubby Anne's shul,
we climb the ancient stairs to the balcony,
where the women are praying,

and we give Bubby Anne
a peck on each cheek
(her cheeks are nice and soft,
not prickly like her husband's).

Then we walk three blocks
to Bubby Etta's shul.
I take Melvin's hand, and we
go up the creaky stairs
to the women's section.

We peek down from the balcony
at the men bowing up and down
and mumbling in Hebrew.

And even though I don't understand
a word of it,
I like hearing the sounds —
it's like a visit with an old friend.

When we find Bubby Etta,
we squeeze over to her seat
and give her kisses, too.

She pats our cheeks
and whispers, *"L'shana tova,"*
warming us up with her smile.

I like the Bubby-kissing part
of our New Year,
even though it's nothing new.

As Long as I'm Here . . .

While I'm in each shul,
I pray to God
that this year I'll figure out
who I am
in this big family of mine.

I don't want to seem greedy,
so I just pray
for a little hint of who
I could possibly be.

I sure wish I knew
if God's listening
to me.

October 2

I wake up today
thinking that maybe this year
Dad'll say something.
But he doesn't.

I act fearless, like Marian,
and run up to him at the door
as he's leaving for the diner.
"It's my birthday today, Dad," I say.
"Oh yeah, how old are you?" he asks.
"Twelve."

Then he pulls some coins
out of his trousers pocket
and counts them into my hands.
"Here are twelve pennies," he says.
He doesn't even say *Happy Birthday,*
but that's okay.

I'll still remember this day always
because it's the first time my dad
has ever given me
anything.

The Dreaded Bee

Ugh,
today's the school spelling bee
and they give me the word,
minuscule.

I ask for its meaning.
"Very small," they say.
Then I sound it out in my head,
m-i-n-i-s-q-u-e-w-e-l-l.

I'm the worst speller
in my class.
Maybe I should just pass.
M-i-n-e-s-c-u-e-l-l.

I'm the worst speller
in school.
And when I spell it out loud —
m-i-n-a-s-k-e-w-e-l,

I feel
just like
my spelling word.

Nobody's Surprised

At the school spelling bee,
nobody's surprised
that the last one standing
is smarty-pants Helen Krashinsky,

and nobody's surprised
that the first one down
is me.

Diner Division

I've missed a lot of lessons at school
because I've been out sick
with whooping cough —
a cough louder than the crash of coal
rumbling down the metal chute
into our cellar.

Now I'm having trouble figuring out
the problem Miss Connelly wrote
on the chalkboard:
How many gallons of gas
can someone buy at nineteen cents a gallon,
if they've got two dollars to spend?

So I turn the math question
into a hot dog problem
because I don't know about gas,
but since I help at Dad's diner sometimes,
I know all about
the price of hot dogs

and I can always figure out
just how many chili dogs
two bucks can buy.

Winter's on Its Way

And I wish I had new shoes
to wear on this rainy day.
But I don't,
so I stuff cardboard
deep down in the soles
of my hand-me-down-downs
and pray I'll get to school
before the rain
soaks through the holes.

A Borrowed Holiday

I love the sparkling lights downtown,
and when I was little,
I loved sitting on Santa's lap,
whispering my wishes
while I was itching to start licking
the candy cane he was going to give me.

Mom has to tear me away from the stores,
where every toy I'd ever want
is crammed into the windows
as tightly as my family in Dad's car.

I love hanging up stockings
on Christmas Eve
and going to bed,
knowing by morning
there'll be tangerines in the toes
and walnuts and filberts and hard candies
and maybe some crayons or jacks
filling up the rest.

And best of all,
I love waking up extra early
to a mound of presents
(there's only one for each,
but with so many of us,
the pile gets pretty high)
and a family stampede.

So when Freddy, a neighbor kid,
says Christmas isn't mine,
I tell him he's wrong:
"Of course it's mine.
Everyone celebrates Christmas."

Then I ask Mom,
and she says it's not really ours,
but we're borrowing it
because here in America
we can celebrate
anything we want.

Another Christmas Morn

Last year
Marian said "Pee yew"
to the green coat she got for Christmas.

Marian said
"Pew yew"
to what Bubby Etta gave her, too.

So this year
Mom filled Marian's stocking
with orange peels and coal.

Now she really
has something
to "Pee yew" about.

My Present

When I unwrap it,
careful not to rip the brown paper
so Mom can reuse it next year,
I find paper dolls inside.

I can't wait to show them to Eunice,
but when I get to her house
and see what she got for Christmas —
roller skates with a shiny key,
a new ruffled dress,
a bingo game,
and a porcelain doll —
I feel like saying "Pee yew"
to my present, too.

The Grass Isn't Always Greener

With our measly presents,
our holey shoes,
our used-up clothes,
and our same old dinner
every Friday night —
matzo ball soup and boiled chicken,

I've been thinking
we're poor . . .

until today,

the day after Christmas,
when our new neighbors,
who have a lot of kids, too,
invite me to stay for dinner.

Their kids got *no* presents at all,
have no shoes on their feet,
and there's nothing in their house to eat
except potatoes and bread

without any butter.

Mildred, Queen of Chocolates

She sits on her throne
while we sit at her feet,
our mouths watering
at the sight of the chocolates
her boyfriend Max gave her for Christmas.

She examines each brown treasure
and with a little push
of her thumb
caves in the bottoms.

She drips
the creams
and caramels
into her own mouth
and shares the nutty ones,
her least favorites,
with us,
her loyal subjects.

I Love Christmas Break

While we're out of school
for Christmas break,
my friends Eunice and Connie and I
run our own little school
for the neighborhood kids
and charge them a penny each.

We teach them how
to make aprons out of burlap
for their mothers,
and pinwheels
out of construction paper and pins.

I wish someday I could be a *real* teacher
like Miss Connelly.
But I stink at spelling
and I don't know
what those big words mean
that smarty-pants Helen Krashinsky uses,
like *preponderance, pungent,* and *pretentious.*

So I guess I'm not smart enough
to be a teacher after all.

Another Plaster Disaster

Christmas break's over
and I'm doing my homework
at the kitchen table
when suddenly chunks of white plaster
rain down on my head.

I look up to see legs
dangling from the ceiling,
and I race up the stairs
to pull Lenny free.

They tell me that Lenny, Sol, and Jack
were all jumping around on the bed
when Lenny missed his step
and fell through the floor.

But Dad's going to go through the roof
when we call the plaster patcher
who's been to our house
fifty times before.

No Plaster Patcher This Time

In the boys' room,
the plastic spacemen
line up on the dresser,
perfect BB-gun targets
for Lenny and Sol.

These crazy brothers of mine cheer
when a BB makes a hit,
and they watch
the little men
as they teeter and fall.

But when Dad goes
to paint their room,
he makes them patch
every one of those
fifty million
holes
in their
bedroom wall.

We Are a Party

I complain to Bubby Etta
about not getting invited
to Passover Seders, weddings,
and bar mitzvahs
because there are too many of us.

She tells me, "*Shayne maideleh,*
you shouldn't worry,
with so many *kinder*
you *are* a party."

I guess she means like when
Mom gives us each a penny
and we go to the A&P across the street,
where Mr. Kennedy fills up bags
with candy and peanuts and pretzels
for each of us.

And when we get home with our bags,
we sit out on the marble steps
and play the movie star guessing game,
giving out only initials as clues,
and we sing our favorite songs
from *Snow White*
while we dig into our bags
and share our treats.

It's a penny candy party,
and with so many of us,
we don't even need to invite
anyone else.

It's Not Always a Party Here, Though

All of us kids are in the cellar clubroom,
crowded around the Victrola,
singing along
to "Some Day My Prince Will Come,"
the song we play over and over
and over again
because we only have three records
and this one's our favorite.

But then Dad stomps downstairs,
yelling, "I told you kids if I heard that song
one more time . . . !"
and he snatches the record
right off the Victrola,
scratching across the voices in mid-song.

He snaps it in two
over his knee.
The little ones start crying.
Even Melvin,
who always has a smile on his face.

And when Melvin looks up
with his chocolate-colored eyes all watery,
I hug him tight.
Now *everyone's* crying,
including me.

Some Things I Just Don't Understand

I can understand
why Dad hollers at us
when we wreck things,
like the ceiling,
because repairs cost money.

And I understand,
because I'm not too bad at math,
that *the Depression + lots of kids = never enough money.*

But I don't understand
why a man who hates children
had twelve of them.
That just doesn't add up.

I'm Not the Performer in the Family

It's Saturday morning,
and Mildred and I
are taking Marian, Annette, Lenny,
Melvin, Sol, and Jack
and the gefilte fish sandwiches
Mom packed for us
to spend the whole day
at the Roxy, watching the cartoons
and the serials and the double feature.

We always try to get to the theater early
so Mildred can perform
in the Kiddie Club onstage
before the movies start.
She sings and tap-dances
so she can win passes
for us to see the movies for free.

I'm glad Mildred has talent,
because if *I* got up there
and tried to sing,
they'd charge us even more
than the regular fifteen-cent admission.

Our Calling Card

On the way to the Roxy
we make our usual stop
to buy sunflower seeds
at the corner pet shop.

I hold hands with Melvin
till we get to a light pole
and we both let go,
yelling, "Crackers and oleo!"

Now we're all watching the Buck Jones serial
and cracking open the seeds with our teeth,
leaving little piles of shells
all around our feet.

But when the ushers clean up
at the end of the show,
they'll never know the shells were ours —
we've all moved down a row.

Now It's Not Too Cold
to Be Outside Anymore

So Mom is making us
scrub and polish
the marble steps
of our row house,
scrub and polish
until they shine.

We rub the sand-soap bars
back and forth
until our arms shake
and those steps sparkle,
all the while muttering
under our breath
about this horrible job
Mom makes us do.

But when the lady next door
offers to pay us each a dime,
we jump at the chance
and polish
hers, too.

Signs of Spring

I know that spring must be here
because, like always
when the weather changes,
there's my big brother Daniel,
propped up in bed with pillows,
wheezing.

And no matter what
the weather's like,
for breakfast
he has to eat his cereal
with water on it.

And worst of all,
he can't have ice cream
or milk shakes
with the rest of us.

But he never, ever complains.
I know *I* would.
Especially about the ice cream.
So I try never to eat any
in front of him.

Our Cousins Are Coming to Town for Passover

They live in New York,
and they must be rich
because Theodora wears Mary Jane shoes
and party dresses all the time,
and Marvin wears long pants
instead of knickers,
and their dad takes family movies
on their very own movie camera.

While they're in Baltimore,
they could stay with Bubby Anne,
who has plenty of room,
or Uncle Willie,
who has a bigger house than ours
and only two kids,
or Uncle Albert,
who has a guest room,
or Aunt Ruth,
who has no kids of her own
and the biggest house of all.
But they always want to stay with us.
It's a mystery to me.

They're the lucky ones
because it's just the two of them,
but they think
squeezing into the beds with us,
where we're already sleeping
three to a bed,
head to foot,
foot to head,
is the greatest thing
ever.

Getting Ready for Passover

Annette is supposed to be scrubbing
the white tile kitchen counters.
But instead she's opening
and slamming cabinets
and rifling through drawers.

I'm busy cleaning out the icebox
with Melvin at my side,
searching for stray bread crumbs
on the kitchen floor,

when Annette comes over to me
all teary-eyed and pitiful.
"I can't find it," she whines.
"Can't find what?" I snap.
"The elbow grease Mom told me to use."

"Keep looking," I tell her,
trying not to laugh.

A Second Chance

Mom brings home
a nice big carp to cook for Passover,
but when Daniel, Mildred, and I see it move,
we decide to save its life.

So we sneak it off the table
and put it in the bathtub,
where it swims around for a while.

But it doesn't really matter.
It still ends up as gefilte fish
served on a silver platter.

Nobody Invites Us to Their House

We'll have the big first-night Passover Seder
at our house,
but only Mom and Dad
are going to Bubby Anne's house
for second-night Seder,
leaving us kids at home,
as usual.

We're always having extra people
at our house for dinner —
Mildred's boyfriends,
Bubby Etta and her husband,
and sometimes our cousins.
Mom doesn't seem to mind —
she just adds more water to the soup.

"I wish somebody
would invite our whole family
to their house for dinner," I tell Daniel.
"It'll never happen," he says.
"It'd be like having
the whole Baltimore Orioles team over."

I guess nobody
wants to have soup
that watery.

A Family Emergency

Connie and Eunice and I
are playing marbles at the corner.
I'm about to roll the shimmy
when Eunice yells, "Hey, Edith,
there's an ambulance by your house
and that looks like your mother getting in."

I race up the street
as the ambulance drives off
with Mom in the back
holding a bundle
wrapped in a blue blanket.
I'm thinking it's the baby.

My stomach churns
as I run up the marble steps to our house.
The door's wide open.
The house is quiet.
But then I hear crying start upstairs.

Baby Sherry's in her crib
and Lenny's standing next to it,
his arm poking through the crib bars,
holding the baby's hand,
and now he's crying so hard
he can't even catch his breath
to answer my questions.

And I'm left wondering
who was wrapped in the blue blanket.

The Worst Night Ever

Dad's lumbering around the parlor,
hunched over like an old man,
and every once in a while
he stops to wrap his arms around Mom,
who's leaving a trail of tissues on the floor
from wiping her red, puffy eyes
and runny nose.

She hands us each a penny
and sends us outside.
"Go buy something
for yourselves," she says.

So we take our pennies
and each other's hands
and trudge to the corner candy store
that stays open until late.

We don't know what to say to one another,
so we just stare at the sidewalk,
and nobody
buys any candy.

Nothing can take away our sadness
on this night when we learned
that we'll never hold hands
with Melvin again.

The Day Our Family Got Too Small

Today
Mom and Dad made me come to school
even though I wanted to be
at Melvin's funeral.

Miss Connelly asks me why I am crying.
I tell her
that the day before yesterday
my little brother Melvin with
his floppy brown ringlets
was wrapping his arms around my legs
like he always does,

that the day before yesterday
he was walking beside me
when I took the baby for a stroll,
keeping his little hands on the carriage,
trying to help me push it.

I tell her that the day before yesterday
my little brother Melvin
had bronchitis
and we didn't know it,
but then all of a sudden
he couldn't breathe,
so Mom took him to the hospital,
and he died there.

And I tell her
that the day before yesterday
I thought my family
was way too big,

but now
my family
is one
too
small.

Melvin's Funeral

Sylvia got to go
because she's the oldest.
She told me how cute he looked
in his white suit
and his yarmulke.

I wasn't allowed to go,
because Mom and Dad
said a cemetery
is no place for children.

If that's true,
then why are they
leaving my little brother there
forever?

It's Passover No Matter What

The funeral was yesterday.
Tonight Passover begins.
Dad says we'll still
have our Passover dinner
even though no one's in the mood.

He brings home a chicken
and tells me to stuff it and cook it.
Mom's too sad to make dinner.
I've watched Mom do it
a million times,
but I've never cooked a chicken myself.

I notice at dinner
that nobody is eating.
"It's much too salty,"
Marian says.

"Eat it anyway," Dad tells us.
"You've lost so much salt
from all the crying."

Sometimes I Forget

Sometimes when I come home from school
I expect Melvin to race to the door
and wrap himself around me
like a snug skirt.

Sometimes when I open the door,
so much noise rushes at me
from Lenny, Sol, Jack, and baby Sherry
that I even think I hear Melvin.

Sometimes when I come in,
someone brushes by me
and I'm sure it's Melvin's floppy curls
I feel tickling my arm.

But then I remember,
and the house
feels too quiet,
too still,
and I can hardly breathe.

It's Shabbos

Mom should be lighting the candles,
but she's not.

She should be pulling in the candlelight
with her hands
just before she covers her eyes
and says the Shabbos blessing,
but she's not.

She should be setting the lit candles
on the dining table
before she serves the meal,
but she's not.

"I cannot thank God
for the Shabbos light
when he has left me
in such darkness," she says.

When God Spoke to Mom

Up until Melvin died,
Mom was working at the diner
while us older kids
were staying home after school
to take care of the younger ones.

But now Mom says
that when Melvin died,
God was telling her
to stay home and be with her children.

So *she's* going to stop working at the diner
and *I* have to start.

I wish *I* could be
one of those children
she's staying home
to be with.

The Meaning of Bittersweet

Mom's in the kitchen
dipping apples in gooey caramel.

She hands me one on a stick
even before the caramel's had a chance to harden.

I ask her if today is a special day,
like maybe somebody's birthday that I forgot.

"Yes, Edith," she says, her voice cracking.
"It is a special day.

"Today we're celebrating the sweetness
that was Melvin."

I bite down hard on the sticky apple,
trying to enjoy its sweetness

while my eyes well up
with bitter tears.

Looking for a Way Out

Every day after school
I walk through the ballpark
on my way to work
at the diner,
and every day
I pray
that one of those balls
will hit me so hard
it'll break some part of me
and I'll get to stop working
and stay home after school and just play
every day.

Back to School with a Plan

Since I haven't gotten hit
by a baseball yet,
I come up with a plan.

I lie and tell Dad
that I've joined lots of clubs
this semester in school —

the Coach Club and Yearbook
and Glee Club
and Farewell Assembly Committee
and Victory Corps–Office Emergency Squad.

I don't know what any of these clubs do,
and I only heard about them
from my big sister Sylvia,
because you have to be in high school
to join them,

but Dad doesn't have to know that.
I'll just tell him I have to stay
so late after school every day,

meeting with all these clubs I've joined,
that I won't have time
to work at the diner.

When I tell Dad
about the clubs,
he scowls at me.

"Clubs, shmubs —
you're too young to join.
You'll work for me after school," he says.

I guess I need a new plan.

A Crime

Now I have an answer for Miss Connelly,
who asked me
at the start of the school year
who I am in this family.

I used to think I was
"the good little mother,"
taking care of my sisters and brothers,
but I'm really
just one of Dad's work slaves.
That's who I am.

Every day after school
I drag myself to the diner,
wishing the police would come
and haul my dad off in chains
for making us kids work all the time.

I wish they'd throw him
into a cold stone cell
and feed him nothing
but lima beans.

And if Dad begged his jailers
to let him out,
to give him another chance
so he could change his ways,
and even promised
never to make any of us kids
work in the diner again,
they'd just sneer at him
and say, "You'd better get used to
lima beans, buddy,
because you're gonna be in here so long
you'll rot!"

Sometimes I Can't Stand Mildred

Before Melvin died
and Mom started staying home,
Sylvia was already working at the diner,
and so were Daniel and Raymond
in between their other jobs,
but not my big sister Mildred.
Even now that Marian and I
have to work there, too,
Mildred still doesn't have to.

She told Dad it would be bad for business
because her many boyfriends
(practically every boy in Baltimore, I think)
would crowd into the restaurant,
sitting around drinking sodas,
taking up tables
just to get a glimpse of her,
and they'd never order a crumb of food.

Maybe Mildred
should work in Bubby Anne's store
since she seems to have a knack
for selling things.
She sold Dad
a bunch of baloney
that he wouldn't have bought
from anybody else.

Working Late

I hate nights like tonight,
when I have to close up the diner
all by myself
because Marian's too young to stay late
and Daniel's working a double shift
at the factory
and Raymond's working
at the service station
and Sylvia's out with her boyfriend
and Mildred never has to work
and Dad is driving his cab.

After I clean off the counters
and put the food away,
I stuff the cash into a brown paper bag,
lock the door, then give it a hard pull
and dash into the black night
with the bag hidden inside my coat.

As I hurry onto the empty bus,
I can feel my heart thumping
like it's going to pop right out of my chest
any minute.

At my stop, I jump off
and race down my street
in case a robber is lurking in the darkness.

And not until I reach the house,
yank the door shut behind me,
and lock it
can I start to breathe again.

The One Good Thing About Working Late

I come home from work
long after midnight,
when the house is silent,
to find a dim light
still on in the kitchen,
and Mom,
with a hot iron in her hand,
working her arm
back and forth,
back and forth
in a rhythm,
and the two of us
talk and talk,
just us,
and I don't
have to share
her

with anyone.

I Need to Know

There's a question that I can't shake
out of my head,
so I use this time alone with Mom
to ask her,
because she always has good answers.

"Remember when you told me
that on Rosh Hashanah
we need to think about the bad things
we've done
and to say we're sorry?

"And remember how you told me
that God decides what will happen
to each of us
in the coming year?"

"Yes, yes," she says. "I remember."

"Since Melvin was too little
to have done anything very bad,
why did God decide to let him die?"
I ask her.

But this time
she doesn't answer.
She just hugs me tight.

I Have a Good Excuse

I can't stay awake in school,
but thank goodness for Eunice,
who pokes me from behind
when it's my turn to read.

Miss Connelly doesn't understand.
She probably thinks I'm lazy.

If only
I could speak up to teachers
like Marian can,
I could tell her that I fall asleep in class
because right after school
I work at Paul's Luncheonette
serving burgers and fries
until the late-night movie closes down
and the ushers come around
for something to eat,
and that I don't get home
till almost 2:00.

If only
Miss Connelly knew.

At the Diner Without Dad

Sylvia, Marian, and I are working today.
Before Dad leaves the diner,
he warns Sylvia,
"Don't let your sisters get into the pies,
you hear me!"

As soon as he walks out the door,
Marian and I ask Sylvia for some pie.
"Sure," she says,
and serves each of us a thick slice.

As that sweet coconut custard
slides across my tongue,
I know that we have the best big sister
of anyone.

Something of My Own

There's this guy we call
Jimmy the Greek
who comes to the diner to eat
whenever I'm working there with Sylvia.

I'm lucky he's sweet on her,
because today
he brought me
a Shirley Temple doll.

It's the first time
I've ever gotten anything
so special that I can truly call
my own.

It almost makes me glad
I'm working
at the diner.

Almost.

I *Had* a Coin Collection

When the soldiers and sailors
come to the diner
they give me coins
from faraway places
to add to my collection.

But today all my coins disappeared,
and I wanted Sol to disappear, too,
when I found out
that he put every one of them
in the pinball machine.

He says he didn't know
they were special.
"I've been saving those coins forever.
Those were mine,
and you had no right
to take them!" I screamed.

I'm awfully glad
that my Shirley Temple doll
is too big to fit
into a pinball machine.

I Can Feel Summer Just Around the Corner

But it won't be like last summer.

Mom will still hang the garden hose
over the clothesline
to make an outdoor shower
for us to run through
on the hottest days,

but Melvin won't be here
to hold my hand
and giggle
when the cool water sprays him.

And Dad will still take us
to the shore on Sundays,

but Melvin won't be here
to hold my hand and squeal
as we play chase with the waves
up and down the beach.

And we'll still stop
on our way home from the shore
for four-cent hot dogs at Hymer's,

but I won't be able
to wipe the mustard and sauerkraut
off his face and fingers and hair.
I won't be able to take his hand
to walk back to the car afterwards.

We never talk about Melvin much
anymore,
but I cry about him
every night in my pillow,
and in the day
my hand feels awfully empty.

An Inspiration

I try to rush out after class
like I always do,
but today Miss Connelly
tells me to stay.

All I can think about
is how she's going to give me detention
for falling asleep in class again,
and how Dad is going to kill me
for being late to work.

But instead,
she asks me in a voice so gentle
it feels like a hug,
"Where do you race off to after school
every day?"

And suddenly the words
start pouring out of me like rain
and I find myself telling her
all about the burgers and diapers
and long days
and late nights
and crowded beds.

Then she says,
"I have seen what you can do
when your eyes are open, Edith.
You're a smart girl and a fast learner, too.
You should go to college someday."

College? Smart? Fast learner?
No one has ever said words
like these to me.
No one.

But then I remember
the girl in my class with the big vocabulary,
and I say, "I don't think I'm so smart,
Miss Connelly.
I don't even know
what any of those big words mean
that Helen Krashinsky uses."

"Neither does she," Miss Connelly says
with a wink.

Floating

I am a bubble
blown full
with Miss Connelly's words,

floating out of the classroom,
bobbing across the grassy lot,
drifting by Levin's Bakery,

letting the breeze carry me to the diner.
"WHERE HAVE YOU BEEN!?"
Dad yells when I come in,

but I just float right by him.

Even Bubbles Have to Work

But at least
I don't have to work the late shift tonight.
So I serve my last hot roast beef sandwich
and float home.

I glide into the parlor.
Do they notice my feet
aren't touching the ground?
"I'm going to college someday,"
I announce,
"and I'm going to be a teacher."

Dad grunts.
"We don't have money for college,
and girls don't need to go anyways,"
he says.
"You'll work at the diner
until you get married."

His words pierce me,
and I burst.

Bubby Comfort

I go over to Bubby Etta's house
to tell her about my future,
the one I had for a little while,
until Dad smashed it into a million pieces.

And even her golden brown knishes
filled with creamy potato
that she's just taken out of the oven
don't help me feel any better.

But then she cradles my cheeks in her hands,
forcing my eyes to look straight into hers,
and says, "Don't worry, *bubbelah*,
you *will* go to college,
and I will help you."

I throw my arms around her
and squeeze her hard,
feeling as if she's just reached
into her shopping bag of gifts
and pulled my dreams out
whole again.

Our Secret

I'm having a late-night ironing talk
with Mom
when I tell her
what Miss Connelly said
about me being smart
and about college
and how Bubby said she'd help.
"That Miss Connelly is a sharp lady,"
Mom says.
Then she leaves the room
and comes back
with something cupped in her hand.
She opens my hand,
drops a wad of dollar bills into it,
and then closes it up tight,
holding her shushing finger
up to her lips.
"For college," she says,
and goes back
to her ironing.

I Have to See for Myself

So I don't tell anyone
where I'm going,
and I take two quarters
(two days' wages)
that I've stashed away
and use them to pay the fare
each way
for two buses
and a trackless trolley.

It takes me
more than an hour
to get there,
but when I do,
it's better than I imagined —

tall brick buildings
with ivy clinging to them,
packed with classrooms and dormitories,
boys and girls
sitting on the grass
in small groups, chatting,
others hurrying down the walkways
hugging their books.

On the way home
I think about how it was definitely
worth two days' wages,
two buses,
and one trolley
to see Towson State Teachers College,
where someday
I'll be going to school.

Who I Am Now

Now I have a better answer
for Miss Connelly,
who wanted me to think about who I am
in my family.

Maybe I am one of Dad's work slaves,
and I'm still
the good little mother,
taking care of my sisters and brothers,
but I am definitely someone else, too.

I am the one
who will go to college someday
and become a teacher.

Maybe He Does Care

We're having a hot-enough-to-fry-eggs-on-
the-pavement
kind of heat wave,
and my whooping cough is so bad
it feels like someone's hammering
on my chest.

It's one in the morning
and I'm sitting on the front steps
coughing nonstop
when Dad comes home from
driving the cab.

"Come on, Edith," he says.
"I'll take you for a ride to cool off."
He rolls all the windows down
and we ride around the neighborhood.

Just me and him.
And I'm not even going to tell him
that I feel a little sick to my stomach
riding in the back seat,

because I don't want anything
to spoil this night
when my dad
is actually being nice

and spending time
just with me.

I Wish

In June I'll be finishing
at McGee Elementary,

but before I go on to junior high
I'm getting an award —
a student achievement award,
the very first in my family.

I wish Mom would come to the ceremony
at McGee,
but she doesn't leave the house much
anymore.

I wish Mom would come —
just for me.

Ironing Out Memories

It's late-night ironing time,
so Mom pulls the board
down from the wall,
stretching a blue blouse over it.

Drops of her tears fall on the shirt
along with the water she sprinkles
before she presses down the iron.

"What's wrong, Mom?" I ask.
"Just thinking about Melvin," she says,
her voice catching on his name.

I wish I knew the right words to say
to help her iron
her sadness away.

No One Will Come to See Me Get My Award

Nobody in my family
has ever gotten a school award
and I'm afraid Mom's too sad to come
and I'm sure Dad doesn't even know
what grade I'm in.

So no one will come see me
get my student achievement award.
No one will clap
when the principal calls my name.
No one will swarm around me
with congratulations and hugs.

What should be my grandest day
will be my saddest
because at least Mom
would have been here,
all dressed in pride.
Mom would have been here
if Melvin hadn't died.

Awards Day, June 2, 1937

Eunice's family is here,
crowding her with hugs and kisses.
She pulls away, beaming,
and we seat ourselves
on the stage.
She's smiling and nodding
at her family of fans,
and I stare
at my hands
folded in my lap . . .

"Edith Paul," the principal calls
in a deep, serious voice.
I walk to the podium
to receive my award,
and out of the blue
I hear an ocean of wild clapping
and whistling.

I look out at the audience
and see them in the back,
grinning and waving,
like a mirage —
Mom, both my *bubbies,* Aunt Ruth,
Sylvia, Daniel, Marian, and all the rest
of my brothers and sisters.

Even
my father.

After My Last Day of School

I go back to McGee,
head down the hall,
find her in the classroom,
boxing up her books,
pulling artwork off the walls,
packing away our whole school year.

"Edith," she says,
"I'm so glad you came by."

Miss Connelly doesn't know
that I couldn't stay away,
that I wish she could be my teacher
forever.

"My mom's giving me money for college,"
I announce.
"That's great news," she says,
stepping right up to me,
closing all the space between us
with a giant hug.

I wish Miss Connelly
could hold me like this
forever.

But I've learned
that there is no forever,
and when she lets go,
I turn to leave quickly
so she won't see
the wetness in my eyes.

She calls to me
as I walk out the door,
"Edith, when you're off at college someday,
I expect to hear from you."

And I go,
knowing I'm on my way
to being so much more
than just plain Edith
who's number four.

AUTHOR'S NOTE

I always knew that I would write the Paul family story one day. *Looking for Me* is a part of that story. My mom, Edith, is the eleven-year-old-turning-twelve narrator, so most of these incidents are based on her memories. Not everything happened exactly as I've written it. For the sake of the story, at times I had to change the roles and ages of some of the characters and fill in the blanks with my own imagination as to what might have taken place.

I collected these stories in my head at first, and later with a mini tape recorder switched on while I pumped my mother and my aunts and uncles for the stories of their childhood. Every adventure, mishap, tragedy, and delight in this book happened in one form or another and involved some member of my mom's enormous, rambunctious family. How do I know? With my relatives, there is no such thing as a quiet family gathering. When my mom and her brothers and sisters get together, they are unstoppable. It doesn't matter how many times we've heard them before, the stories flow until they flood the room. Since each of the brothers and sisters has a slightly different take on every story, like in the game of telephone, many of these tales, through their telling, have changed over the years.

Edith, "the little mother," eventually grew up to become an extraordinary mother to my brother and me. And in case you're wondering, she did end up going to college, the only girl in her family to do so. Her brother Danny, who went to college on the GI Bill after serving in the military, was the only other Paul child to earn a college degree.

Since the surviving eleven siblings all went on to marry and have children of their own (no more than three each), I have dozens and dozens of cousins. I count myself lucky to be so rich in family.

Edith Paul

GLOSSARY

auction: The Paul family was able to keep its home because of the Home Owners' Loan Corporation, founded in 1933 under President Franklin D. Roosevelt, which helped homeowners keep their homes and avoid foreclosure during the Depression.

bubbelah: Yiddish term of endearment meaning "darling."

challah: Special egg bread, often braided, eaten by Jews on the Sabbath and holidays.

crackers and oleo!: During World War II, instead of saying "bread and butter" when hand-holders were separated by something coming between them, they'd say "crackers and oleo" because of the shortage and increased cost of butter. Oleo is margarine, a butter substitute.

gefilte fish: Poached fish patties made from a mixture of ground fish, mostly carp or pike. A traditional food typically eaten by Ashkenazi Jews on the Sabbath and holidays.

kinder: Yiddish for "children."

kishkes: Slang for "guts."

knishes: Baked or fried turnovers filled with potato or meat or cheese.

l'shana tova: A greeting used on Rosh Hashanah, the Jewish New Year, meaning "to a good year."

mezuzah: A small parchment scroll inscribed with biblical passages in Hebrew and inserted in a case. The case is attached by Jewish households to their doorposts, as required by Jewish law and as a sign of their faith.

milkhikh: Yiddish for "dairy." The kosher laws forbid the mixing of meat and dairy.

pirogen: Small pastry turnovers with a filling. Can be made sweet or be filled with things like chopped meat or mashed potatoes.

potato latkes: Potato pancakes.

Rosh Hashanah: The Jewish New Year, which follows the lunar calendar, usually occurs in September or October.

schmaltz: Rendered (melted) animal fat, usually chicken fat. Often used in Eastern European–style Jewish cooking.

Seder: "Order" in Hebrew. The Passover Seder is a Jewish ritual feast that marks the beginning of the Jewish holiday of Passover.

Shabbos: The Yiddish word for the Jewish Sabbath, which begins on Friday night and concludes at sundown on Saturday night.

shayne maideleh: In Yiddish, "pretty girl."

shul: Synagogue.

Workmen's Circle Lodge or Arbeter Ring: A national organization founded in 1900 by progressive-minded immigrants to promote Jewish community, Jewish culture, and social justice.

yarmulke: The skullcap worn in synagogue by Jewish males and worn every day by Orthodox Jewish men.

zayde: Yiddish for "grandfather." Jacob is Edith's step-grandfather.

zhyd: Pronounced *zid*. Russians used this word as an offensive term for Jews and enemies alike.

ACKNOWLEDGMENTS

Most of all I'd like to thank my mom for digging deep into her past to patiently answer my constant questions, and her many siblings for telling their stories to me (and anyone else who would listen) over and over and over again. If not for Edith, Sylvia, Mildred, Danny, Raymond, Marian, Annette, Melvin, Lenny, Sol, Jack, and Sherry, *Looking for Me* would not be. And I thank them, as well, for all the love and laughter that accompanied those stories. Unknowingly perhaps, all of them set me on the path to becoming a writer.

My dad, too, was instrumental in my choice of careers. I thank him for teaching me that good writing is the key to unlocking many doors.

Sonya Sones and Ann Wagner have seen the poems for this book so many times that they must have all the lines memorized by now. I thank them from the bottom (and the top) of my heart for their continuously insightful input. The Society of Children's Book Writers and Illustrators deserves my undying gratitude for awarding me a Work-in-Progress Grant for *Looking for Me*. If not for the grant, this manuscript might not have gotten into the capable hands of Erica Zappy, who was one of the grant judges and subsequently became the editor of this book. Thanks go to SCBWI for paving the way, and to Erica for her enthusiastic embrace of my story.

Last, but not least of course, I want to thank my husband, David, for being my biggest cheerleader, and my three kids, Adam, Sara, and Joel, for giving me a small taste of the fulfillment my grandmother found and the challenges she faced raising twelve children.

Minnie Paul holding Danny. Sam Paul holding Mildred (left) and Sylvia (right) in front of their row house in Baltimore.

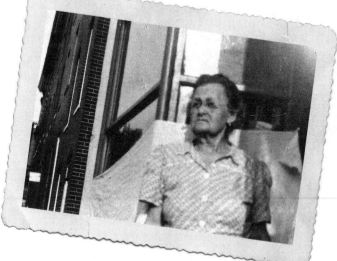

Bubby Anna

Minnie holding Sherry.

Sol, Sherry, and Jack, from left to right.

Sol in front of the family diner.